W9-AAK-819

Other Books by Mitsumasa Anno
Published by Philomel Books:

All in a Day (by Mitsumasa Anno et alia)
Anno's Britain
Anno's Counting House
Anno's Flea Market
Anno's Hat Tricks
Anno's Journey
Anno's Medieval World
Anno's Mysterious Multiplying Jar
Anno's Peekaboo
Anno's Sundial
Socrates and the Three Little Pigs (text by Tuyosi Mori)
Upside-Downers

First USA edition 1983. Published by Philomel
Books, a division of The Putnam & Grosset Group,
200 Madison Avenue, New York, NY 10016.
Originally published in 1983 by Fukuinkan Shoten
Publishers, Tokyo as *Tabi No Ehon IV* by
Mitsumasa Anno, copyright © 1983 by Kuso-kobo.
Published simultaneously in Canada. Sandcastle
Books and the Sandcastle logo are trademarks
belonging to The Putnam & Grosset Group. All
rights reserved. Printed in Singapore.

Library of Congress Cataloging in Publication Data
Anno, Mitsumasa, Anno's U.S.A.
Translation of: Tabi no ehon, IV.
Summary: In wordless panoramas a lone traveler
approaches the New World from the West
in the present day and journeys the width
of the country backward through time,
departing the east coast as the Santa Maria
appears over the horizon.
[1. United States—Pictorial works. 2. Stories
without words.] I. Title
PZ7.A5875As 1983   [Fic]   833-13107
ISBN 0-399-20974-3
ISBN 0-399-21595-6 (pbk)
First Sandcastle Books Impression
Third hardcover impression

ANNO'S U.S.A.

Mitsumasa Anno

PHILOMEL BOOKS
NEW YORK

A traveler, arriving on the West Coast of the United States, journeyed on toward the East. Along the way, he stopped in many villages, towns and cities; he saw ghost towns — towns that had been built around now-deserted gold or silver mines; he also visited the scenes of long-ago battles. In Alabama he talked with an elderly man who was working in a cotton patch; in old New Orleans he met some young boys tap-dancing. In the forest wilderness in Kansas and in the deserts of New Mexico he passed by pioneers who were venturing to the West in their covered wagons. In Hannibal, Missouri, he had the good fortune to meet Tom Sawyer and his friends, whom he had been most eager to draw.

The history of America has progressed generally from the East to the West; therefore the traveler who went in the opposite direction felt as though he were turning back the pages of time, one by one. At the last, when he was leaving the Atlantic shore of North America, he met the *Mayflower* arriving — something that had happened more than three hundred years ago! And he glimpsed the *Santa Maria*, Christopher Columbus's flagship, just coming over the horizon.

While rowing home in his own small boat, the traveler recalled with many thanks all the kindnesses the people he met during his journey had shown to him. I will be happy if you can share these people's kind hearts with him as you read this book.

— Mitsumasa Anno

Afterword

As a child in Tsuwano, a small town in western Japan, Mitsumasa Anno felt an intense curiosity about the ocean that lay beyond the mountains surrounding the green and beautiful valley in which he lived. When, at the age of ten, he finally made the journey to the ocean, he immediately began to wonder about the countries across the sea.

In 1963 he made his first visit to Europe, a visit that resulted ultimately in his book *Anno's Journey*. Since then, with sketchbook and camera in hand, he has made several more trips to Europe and the British isles, recording his observations in *Anno's Italy* and *Anno's Britain*. A brief trip to the United States in 1977 opened his eyes to the wonders of the New World, and he returned in the autumn of 1981 for a longer stay.

Already familiar with America's art, literature and history, as well as its famous children's books, its films and folklore, Mr. Anno arrived with some idea of what he wanted to see, and a preconceived notion of how he would proceed. As he had done in Europe and in Britain, he planned to rent a car and simply drive at leisure from one end of the country to the other, inviting serendipitous views, events and insights. But the immense scale of America's geography came as a shock, as it often does to newcomers to its shores. Nevertheless, he managed to cover an astonishing amount of territory according to his original plan, exploring bustling cities and quiet country byways at his own pace, savoring the special qualities of each part of the United States and its richly mixed population.

As always in his journeying, he preferred the woods and green fields, the mountains and fertile farmlands, but he also visited the cities with their striking architecture and their busy inhabitants. Only Anno could find a way to show modern New York City without cars! The city's streets are filled, not with traffic, but with an exuberant parade, featuring the Wild Things from Maurice Sendak's beloved book; Paul Bunyan and his famous blue ox, "Babe"; the New York Public Library's lions; and a sculpture of the traveler himself on his horse, among many other things.

"I want my readers to work to discover for themselves as many as they can of the points I have illustrated," declares Mr. Anno. "And I hope this gives them as much pleasure (and as many problems) as it did me in putting ideas together on the pages." Hidden amid the trees in New York's Central Park are a variety of animals presumably escaped from the Zoo. In scenes set in other areas of the country, the sharp-eyed (and sharp-witted) viewer can spy George Caleb Bingham's *Fur Traders Descending the Missouri*, Grant Wood's *American Gothic*, Edward Hicks's *The Peaceable Kingdom*, and famous paintings by Winslow Homer, James McNeill Whistler, Andrew Wyeth, Tasha Tudor and many more; scenes from film epics like *Gone With the Wind*, *She Wore a Yellow Ribbon*, and *Shane*; characters from *Uncle Tom's Cabin*, *Tom Sawyer*, and *Little Women*; childhood favorites like Marie Hall Ets's *Play With Me*, Uri Shulevitz's *Dawn*, Laura Ingalls Wilder's "Little House" books, Marjorie Flack's *Angus and the Ducks* and Robert McCloskey's *Make Way for Ducklings*; landmarks like the Alamo, the Old State House in Boston, Preservation Hall in New Orleans, Washington's Capitol Building, the Governor's Palace in Williamsburg, and Independence Hall in Philadelphia. Cattle ranches, cotton plantations, Indian pueblos, cornfields and backyard gardens and dozens of other aspects of the vast and varied American scene are depicted in fascinating detail in Mr. Anno's delicate watercolor-and-ink technique. In all, Mitsumasa Anno blends the liveliness of the present with the loveliness of the past, subtly but unmistakably making his point that we must appreciate and preserve our natural environment. "Human beings can't live without nature," Mr. Anno has said. "No human beings can really live without earth and grass and sky." In this book, he celebrates the vigor and ingenuity of the people and the beauty of the magnificent natural scenery of the U.S.A.